E   Disher, Garry.
           Switch cat.

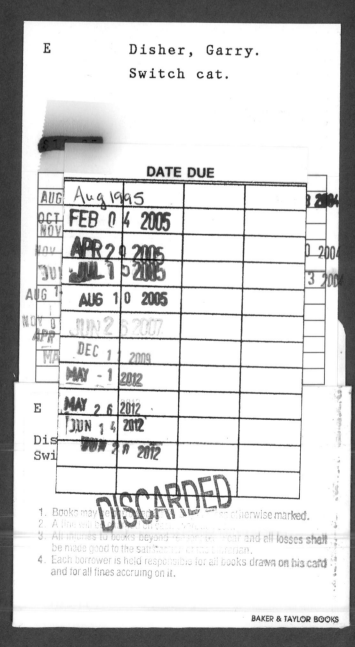

DATE DUE			
Aug 1995			
FEB 0 4 2005			
APR 2 9 2005			
JUL 1 5 2005			
AUG 1 0 2005			
JUN 2 6 2007			
DEC 1 1 2009			
MAY - 1 2012			
MAY 2 6 2012			
JUN 1 4 2012			
JUN 2 8 2012			

E

Dis

Swi

1. Books may be kept for two weeks unless otherwise marked.
2. A fine will be charged on each book which is not returned on time.
3. All injuries to books beyond reasonable wear and all losses shall be made good to the satisfaction of the librarian.
4. Each borrower is held responsible for all books drawn on his card and for all fines accruing on it.

SWITCH CAT

by Garry Disher
illustrated by Andrew McLean

Ticknor & Fields Books for Young Readers
New York 1995

Text copyright © 1994 by Garry Disher
Illustrations copyright © 1994 by Andrew McLean

First American edition 1995 published by
Ticknor & Fields
Books for Young Readers
A Houghton Mifflin company, 215 Park Avenue South, New York, New York 10003.

First published in Australia by Ashton Scholastic Pty Limited

Manufactured in the United States
Book design by Mina Greenstein
The text of this book is set in 16 pt. Zapf International Medium
The illustrations are colored pencils, water colors, and guoache, reproduced in full color

BVG 10 9 8 7 6 5 4 3 2 1

Library of Congress Cataloging in Publication Data
Disher, Garry.
Switch Cat / by Garry Disher; illustrated by Andrew McLean.—1st American ed.
      p.   cm.
Summary: Two cats and their owners have mismatched personalities.
ISBN 0-395-71643-8
[1. Cats—fiction. 2. Moving, Household—Fiction. 3. Stories in rhyme.]
I. McLean, Andrew, ill.   II. Title.
PZ8.3.D615Sw 1995 [E]—dc20 94-21002   CIP   AC

For Lucy
— G. D.

For Megan, Emily, and Andrew,
Michael and Ben
— A. M.

Look at me:
scabby knees,
a voice that squeaks,
handwriting like a puddled street.

Frenzied hair
six days a week,
mismatched socks upon my feet.
No wonder I offend . . .

Evangelina.
Look at her:
supple,
proud,
satiny,
sleek,

slipping next door,
black and fleet.
It's clear to me that she prefers . . .

Cecilia.
Swanlike in her dancing shoes,
expert on the computer,
well informed about the news,
no apple cores, no clutter.

It's no surprise that she offends . . .

Ms. Whiz.
Scruffy,
torn,
fishbreathy,
mean,

a mad-eyed spark
on the trunks of trees.

Grubby,
worn,
sunloving,
lean,

trample-purring
around my knees.

It's clear to me where Whiz
prefers to live.

But our parents say, "You must be firm!"
I hear it so often, it's boring,
yet it's no use saying "Scoot!" at night

if I'm smack-door'd awake in the morning.

Or "Stay here, Ev," with all my might,

if I'm deafened by caterwauling.

And both cats know when it's bedtime,

and both are good at stalling.

But one day Whiz was there no more.
This is how it happened:
awoken by a noise next door,
I drew back the curtain,
saw cartons, crates, rugs from the floor,
moving vans and workmen,

a loaded car,
a clawing paw,
Whiz snarling,
"This is rotten!"

I can't exist without her,
I miss her day and night;
sometimes I think I hear her,
ready to pounce and bite;

sometimes I think I see her,
crouched on the edge of sight.
But when I look, it's never her,
it's just a trick of the light.

And poor Evangelina,
face pressed to the glass,

yearning for Cecilia,
yearning for the past.

So it's Ev's heart, Whiz's heart,
Cecilia's heart, mine.
Every day I count them,
every day I pine,
hopscotching broken hearts,
one hop at a time—

until I am Whiz-tangled,
and I step on a line!

She's journeyed far to be with me,
so no more questions, please.
Let her rest her weary bones,
and snuffle-growl for fleas.

Imagine all that she's been through:
she's crossed deserts and climbed trees,
been chased through swollen rivers,
by wolfhounds, geese, and bees.

But I want you all to notice,
I want you all to see:
Ev now lives with Cecilia,
and Whiz lives here with me.